Happy Birthday,
Grambo,

For your birthday,
Pasta and I are
sending another Hawaiian
story book for your
library.

We love you
so much,
Boobie
&
Pasta

9 April 2006

# The Surf Rats
## of
# Waikīkī Beach

### Carmen Geshell
### Illustrated by Jeff Pagay

Design: Carol Colbath
Copyright © 2004 by Bess Press, Inc.
ALL RIGHTS RESERVED
Printed in Korea
ISBN: 1-57306-226-X

3565 Harding Avenue
Honolulu, Hawai'i 96816
phone: (808) 734-7159
fax: (808) 732-3627
e-mail: sales@besspress.com
http://www.besspress.com

This is a story about a rascal bunch of rodents who nearly took over Waikīkī Beach. Part of it is true, and the rest of it is jus' plain fun. So sit back, stick your toes in the sand, and have yourself one plenny good time.

The Surf Rats, as they called themselves, lived in the great banyan tree on the famous O'ahu beach. It was the perfect spot for them. They loved the ocean, the bustling tourist action, and most of all the statue of their surfing hero, Duke Kahanamoku.

Their leader was Da Big Kahuna. He was the oldest and the best surfer of them all. He also played sweet tunes on his trusty ukulele.

Sistah Tuni was a sassy-kine rat with a good heart. When she wasn't catching a wave, she could be found singing *hapa-haole* songs for anyone who would listen.

Rasta was a quiet and thoughtful rat. Good at making things, Rasta shaped surfboards like a pro—not to mention guitars, which he loved to play at night.

Shaka was the most fearless wave-rider of them all. Surfing was his life, and it showed. (Psst, confidentially, we think he's wiped out one too many times!) He'd also been playing the bongos ever since he was a little pup.

Sweetie, the youngest of the group, was an excellent grom who played a wicked bass.

As you have probably learned by now, the Surf Rats enjoyed music as much as riding the waves. Often they could be found jamming together at night beneath the banyan tree, working for tips of shiny pennies and donations of leftover bentos from generous passers-by.

Surfing by day and playing tunes all night sounds pretty good, doesn't it? Well, the Surf Rats sure thought so. So much so, in fact, that after a while, things got a little out of hand. Da Big Kahuna nibbled on beachgoers' musubi. Sistah Tuni found it great fun changing people's radio dials. Rasta smashed into *keiki*'s sand castles as he ran to catch a wave. Shaka hitched rides on tourists' air mattresses as they floated in the shallow aqua water. And Sweetie used the lifeguard tower as her own personal afternoon nap spot.

The five-some seemed more like five hundred, as the rats ran here, there, and all ovah creation!

Things got so bad that Da Mayah of Honolulu decided to check things out. Because you see, tourists and locals alike were mighty upset. And rightly so. Da Mayah witnessed the rats' *kolohe* ways firsthand when Shaka ran right up his leg!

Right then and there, Da Mayah decided that something must be done. People came from all over the globe to visit Waikīkī Beach. If things continued the way they were going, no one would have any fun.

The Surf Rats had to go! An eviction notice was posted on their tree the very next day.

That night, the Surf Rats' instruments were silent. Instead of jamming, all the rats gathered inside the old banyan. As always, Da Big Kahuna was front and center.

"What are we going to do?" asked Sistah Tuni.

"Will we have to move?" Rasta quietly asked. He hated the idea of leaving the beach and living at the landfill. Or worse yet, in the sewer!

"I'd love to live on Mars!" Shaka joined in. "Can we go there?"

Sweetie and the others just rolled their eyes. There was no surfing on that big red rock in outer space!

Da Big Kahuna tapped his toe and felt his whiskers. This was one major-kine *pilikia*. "Maybe da big guy is right," he said of Da Mayah. "Maybe we have gone a bit gonzo. But that doesn't mean we can't change, do better. Come closer, guys. I have a plan that might work."

Bright and early that next morning, the Surf Rats donned their best aloha wear and headed for City Hall, hoping to meet with Da Mayah.

Luckily, Da Mayah was a kind-hearted guy who liked animals. He agreed to meet with the Surf Rats. Newspeople from all over town came as well. All were eager to hear what would be decided at Honolulu Hale that day.

15

The rats loved their home and wanted to stay. Da Mayah wanted the best for his people. A compromise was needed.

"All I'm asking for is a little *kōkua*, a little hospitality, and a lot of aloha spirit," Da Mayah told them. "If you think you can give me that, then we have a deal."

"But how?" Sweetie piped up. She was just a little rat, and Da Mayah looked so big.

"Think of what Duke would do," said Da Mayah.

The Surf Rats looked at each other and smiled. With the image of their idol, Duke Kahanamoku, in their five little heads, they knew just what Da Mayah had in mind.

"Mistah Mayah," began Tuni. "You've got yourself one sweet deal!"

A week later the Surf Rats proved that they were as good as their word. Da Big Kahuna offered his expert advice about local grinds to hungry *malihini*. Sistah Tuni helped sunbathers find music they liked on the radio. Rasta carried buckets of water and helped the *keiki* build bigger and better sandcastles. Shaka helped blow up air mattresses instead of riding on them. And Sweetie now took her afternoon nap in the cool shade beneath the life-guard tower. You could really say that they had cleaned up their act and played a new tune altogether.

And whenever they needed inspiration, all they had to do was look at the statue of the famous surf legend and much-loved ambassador of aloha. For you see, Duke loved people, not to mention sharing the joys of sun, sand, and sea, and the music of the islands.

The Surf Rats combined all that in their plan. And they did so by helping folks learn to surf, play ukulele, paddle outrigger canoes, and dance the hula, just like back in the days when the Waikīkī beach boys were kings!

Everyone was pleased. Visitors to the beach were happy to have a harmonious place to relax. The Surf Rats were more than happy to keep the home they loved so much. And perhaps the happiest of them all was Da Mayah. Why? Because EVERYONE was happy.

"Good job, guys. Way to go!" he told the Surf Rats one day.

"T'anks, brah," smiled Da Big Kahuna.

Da Mayah smiled too. "Just one more thing."

All the Surf Rats looked worried. Except for Shaka. He still wanted to visit Mars.

"What is it, Mayah?" Rasta bravely asked.

22

"Do you think you could teach ME to surf?"

The rats huddled together and talked it over in secret whispers. Then they gave Da Mayah their answer.

"Shuah," smiled Da Big Kahuna once again. "We can do that. After all, it's what Duke would have done."

23

# Glossary

**bento: (Japanese)**   typically, a boxed meal or a plate lunch.

**brah (Pidgin)**   brother, guy, dude.

**Duke Kahanamoku**   (1890–1968) Known as the Father of International Modern Surfing, Duke Paoa Kahanamoku was also a champion swimmer, winning medals at four Olympic Games. For many years he was Hawai'i's official Ambassador of Aloha, and today is a world-renowned icon of the Hawaiian Islands and a hero not only to the Surf Rats, but to us all.

**gonzo (surfer-speak)**   enthusiastic. Or in the Surf Rats' case, over-enthusiastic.

**grinds (Pidgin)**   food.

**grom (surfer-speak)**   a young surfer, also known in California as a "rat."

**hapa-haole music**   a style of music popular during the "boat days" of the early to mid-1900s. It is often sung in a falsetto style and accompanied by a steel guitar. Its name combines the Hawaiian words hapa (part) and haole (Caucasian person).

**kahuna (Hawaiian)**   priest, minister, sorcerer, or expert in any profession.

**keiki (Hawaiian)**   child, children.

**kōkua (Hawaiian)**   help, aid.

**kolohe (Hawaiian)**   mischievous, naughty.

**malihini (Hawaiian)**   stranger, newcomer, guest.

**musubi (Japanese)**   rice ball, sometimes with ume (pickled plum) inside.

**pilikia (Hawaiian)**   trouble of any kind.

**shaka (Pidgin)**   Hawaiian hand gesture consisting of a fist with raised thumb and pinky finger, used as a symbol of goodwill and happy tidings. Hang loose, brah!

**sistah (Pidgin)**   sister, girl, lady.

**ukulele**   small guitar-shaped musical instrument brought to Hawai'i from Portugal in 1879. In Hawaiian it means "leaping flea."

**Waikīkī (Hawaiian)**   world-famous beach and tourist area on the island of O'ahu. Literally means "spouting water."

For Natalie Stevens, who is also known as Nat the Rat, and my rascal kitty, Nohea Girl

C. G.

To all those who show the aloha spirit to our visitors, *mahalo!*

J. P.